Big L

by

Liane Moriarty

A 30-minute Instaread Summary

Please Note

This is an unofficial summary. We encourage you to purchase the full book if you have not already.

Copyright © 2014 by Instaread Summaries. All rights reserved worldwide. No part of this publication may be reproduced or transmitted in any form without the prior written consent of the publisher.

Limit of Liability/Disclaimer of Warranty: The publisher and author make no representations or warranties with respect to the accuracy or completeness of these contents and disclaim all warranties such as warranties of fitness for a particular purpose. The author or publisher is not liable for any damages whatsoever. The fact that an individual or organization is referred to in this document as a citation or source of information does not imply that the author or publisher endorses the information that the individual or organization provided. This concise summary is unofficial and is not authorized, approved, licensed, or endorsed by the original book's author or publisher.

Contents

Book Overview 5
Main Characters 15
Chapter Summaries & Key Happenings 20
Chapters 1-4 21
Chapters 5-8 24
Chapters 9-12 28
Chapters 13-16 32
Chapters 17-20 36
Chapters 21-24 39
Chapters 25-28 44
Chapters 29-32 48
Chapters 33-36 53
Chapters 37-40 57
Chapters 41-44 61
Chapters 45-48 64
Chapters 49-52 68
Chapters 53-56 73
Chapters 57-60 76
Chapters 61-64 80
Chapters 65-68 84
Chapters 69-72 88
Chapters 73-76 93
Chapters 77-80 98
Chapters 81-84 103

A Reader's Perspective 108

Book Overview

Big Little Lies by Liane Moriarty, set in Australia, tells the story of three very different mothers who form an unusual friendship. The women are first drawn together because their children are all in the same kindergarten class. The women become friends while each struggles with her own secrets and family problems.

Jane Chapman first meets Madeline Mackenzie as they are on their way to kindergarten orientation. Jane is a single mom to son Ziggy. She is trying to be a good mother while dealing with her past.

Madeline introduces Jane to her friend Celeste White at the local coffee shop.

Madeline Mackenzie has two children with her second husband, Ed. Her daughter, Chloe, is in the same kindergarten class as Jane's son, Ziggy. She also has a fourteen-year-old daughter named Abigail with her ex-husband, Nathan. Nathan is remarried to a younger woman named Bonnie. Nathan and Bonnie have a daughter named Skye who is also in kindergarten. Madeline is jealous of the time Abigail spends with Nathan and Bonnie, afraid she is losing her to them.

Celeste White is married to Perry White, and they have twin sons named Josh and Max who are also in kindergarten. Celeste and Perry are wealthy, beautiful and appear to have a happy marriage. Perry is a good father and family man. He is attentive and generous to Celeste, but he also has a dark side. He abuses Celeste behind closed doors. However, she stays with him for their sons.

At kindergarten orientation, Ziggy is accused of choking another student, Amabella, the daughter of Renata Klein. Ziggy denies hurting Amabella, but Renata does not believe him. Once school starts, Amabella is again hurt by one of her classmates, but she will not say who it is. Renata assumes it is Ziggy. Madeline, who is already a rival of Renata's, and Celeste side with Jane in defending Ziggy against Renata's accusations.

A petition is started and passed around the school demanding Ziggy be suspended. This petition is a source of controversy among the parents at the school. Some parents tell their children that they are not allowed to play with Ziggy. Ziggy continues to deny hurting Amabella. Jane believes that Ziggy is innocent, but she is worried.

Celeste continues to be abused by Perry. After an episode of abuse, she goes to see a domestic abuse counselor. The counselor advises her to form an escape plan because Perry will hit her again, and she needs to be prepared to get away from him. Celeste secretly rents and furnishes an apartment for her and her sons so that it is ready in case she decides to leave Perry.

Madeline has a conflict with her daughter when Abigail decides she would rather live with her father and her stepmother than with Madeline and Ed. Madeline feels hurt and abandoned. She thinks she cannot compare with the younger and seemingly perfect Bonnie.

Jane tells both Madeline and Celeste, separately, the story of the one night stand that led to Ziggy's conception. After going out drinking with friends, Jane went to a hotel with a strange man who told her his name was Saxon Banks. Although she intended to have sex with him, she was shocked and frightened when he tried to choke her. He then had sex with her while degrading her for her looks. Celeste knows Saxon Banks. He is her husband's cousin.

Tension is high the night of the school trivia night. It is a costume event with parents and teachers dressed up as either Elvis Presley or Audrey Hepburn. Perry has found out about Celeste's secret apartment. She tells him that she is going to leave him the next week while he is away on a trip. Both Jane and Celeste have found out that the school bully is not Ziggy. It is one of Celeste's sons, Max. Celeste also learns Max has also started bullying Nathan and Bonnie's daughter, Skye.

At the trivia night, most of the parents and teachers are drunk on cocktails that were accidentally made too strong. Arguments and fights break out. Jane is introduced for the first time to Celeste's husband, Perry. When he takes off his Elvis wig, she is shocked to see that he is the man with whom she had the one night stand. When she tells him that she has met him before but his name then was Saxon Banks, Celeste realizes that Perry posed as his cousin, and he is actually Ziggy's father. She throws her drink at him, and he hits her. The others jump in to protect Celeste.

Bonnie realizes that Perry has abused Celeste before and his children have seen him do it. She thinks this is why Max has become a bully. Although no one else but Nathan knows, Bonnie is the daughter of an abusive father, and she snaps when she realizes the truth about Perry. She shoves him off the bar stool he is sitting on, and he falls over the balcony and dies. She did not mean to kill him. At first the others on the balcony plan to hide the truth about what happened to Perry in order to protect Bonnie, but she decides to confess so they will not have to lie for her. Bonnie is sentenced to community service instead of jail time.

Celeste sells her house and she moves to the apartment with her sons. Jane starts dating Tom, the owner of Blue Blues, the local coffee shop.

Main Characters

Madeline Mackenzie: Madeline Mackenzie is married to her second husband and has two children with him plus a third child with her first husband. She is trying to deal with the problems of a blended family while at the same time helping her friends and handling ongoing rivalries with others.

Jane Chapman: Jane Chapman is a single mother of one son. She is new to town and is trying to move on from her troubled past.

Celeste White: Celeste White is beautiful, wealthy, and the mother to twin boys. Although by all appearances she is happily married to her husband, Perry, their relationship is actually one of domestic abuse and hidden secrets.

Perry White: Perry White is Celeste's husband. He is handsome, rich and seems to be a good family man, but his private life includes spousal abuse and infidelity.

Nathan: Nathan is Madeline's ex-husband and father to Abigail. He was not around for Abigail during her growing up years, but he is trying to make up for his past by being a better father to Abigail and to his daughter, Skye, whom he had with his second wife, Bonnie.

Bonnie: Bonnie is Nathan's second wife and the mother to Skye. Madeline finds her annoying because she does yoga, is vegan, promotes peace, does charity work, and is always nice to everyone.

Abigail Mackenzie: Abigail Mackenzie is the teenage daughter of Madeline and Nathan. She has to deal with living in a blended family and learn to make the right choices as she goes from being no longer a child to not quite an adult.

Ziggy Chapman: Ziggy Chapman is the five-year-old son of Jane Chapman. As the product of a one night stand, he is without a father and is ostracized in kindergarten when it is said that he is a bully.

Max White: Max White is one of Celeste and Perry White's twin sons. As a witness to domestic abuse in his home between his mother and father, Max becomes an abuser himself when he bullies girls in his kindergarten class.

Amabella Klein: Amabella Klein is the classmate to the children of Madeline, Celeste, and Jane. She becomes the center of a controversy at her school when she accuses Ziggy Chapman of bullying her.

Chapter Summaries & Key Happenings

Chapters 1-4

Mrs. Patty Ponder, an elderly woman who lives next to the Pirriwee Public School in Pirriwee Beach, Australia, hears a commotion going on at the school's trivia night. She looks out the window and sees fighting going on among the parents at the event. She hears a woman screaming.

Madeline Mackenzie drives her daughter, Chloe, to her kindergarten orientation day at school. When she comes to a stop light, Madeline gets out of her car and goes to the car in front of her to yell at a woman who is using her phone while driving. On the way back to her car, Madeline turns her ankle and falls.

Newcomers to the area, Jane Chapman and her son, Ziggy, are in the car behind Madeline. They are also on their way to kindergarten orientation. Jane sees Madeline fall and gets out of her car to help her.

Jane gets Ziggy and Chloe to the school, then she and Madeline go to Blue Blues, a beachside café, to meet Madeline's friend, Celeste. Madeline tells Jane about her ex-husband, Nathan, and his new family. Jane tells Madeline that she is a single mom. She says Ziggy is the result of a one-night stand.

Key Happening

- Single mother Jane Chapman meets Madeline Mackenzie and Celeste White when their children go to kindergarten orientation. The three mothers meet for coffee at Blue Blues, a beachside cafe.

Chapters 5-8

At the café, Madeline tells Celeste and Jane about some of the other kindergarten mothers.

While waiting for the children to be dismissed from orientation, Jane meets Renata, who is somewhat of a rival to Madeline. Amabella, Renata's daughter, comes out of the school crying. She accuses Ziggy of choking her. Ziggy claims he did not do it.

Renata and the kindergarten teacher, Miss Barnes, ask Ziggy to apologize to Amabella. He states again that he did not do anything. Jane stands up for Ziggy saying that he does not lie. Madeline steps in to try and smooth things over. Renata tells her to stay out of it and then tells Ziggy he will regret it if he touches Amabella again.

Madeline and her husband, Ed, get up on Christmas morning and are about to open gifts with their children, Fred and Chloe, when Madeline gets a text from her daughter, Abigail. Abigail is the daughter she had in her first marriage with Nathan. Abigail tells Madeline that she is helping prepare a meal at the homeless shelter with Nathan and Bonnie, her stepmother. Madeline resents the time that Abigail spends with Nathan and his family.

She is jealous when it seems that Abigail chooses being with them over being with her.

Key Happenings

- Amabella Klein, another student at the orientation, claims that Jane's son, Ziggy, hurt her, but Ziggy denies it. Amabella is the daughter of Renata, one of Madeline's rivals.

- On Christmas morning, Madeline resents it when her daughter Abigail chooses to spend time with her ex-husband Nathan and his new wife Bonnie.

Chapters 9-12

Celeste White and her husband, Perry, who are very wealthy, fly with their two sons, Josh and Max, from their home in Australia to Canada so they can have snow for Christmas. From the outside, it appears they are very happy. However, things are not as they appear because Perry hits Celeste.

Jane wakes up on Christmas morning from a nightmare she is having that Ziggy has his foot on her throat and she cannot breathe. She is reminded of a bad memory from her past. She worries that

Ziggy might have inherited violent tendencies from his father.

Celeste and Perry fly back to Australia with their sons. Celeste notices how handsome Perry looks and is reminded of how attracted she is to him. Perry tells her that he is going to try to make it a good year for them.

Chloe asks if she can have a playdate with Ziggy. Abigail thinks Chloe should have a playdate with her step sister, Skye, instead. Madeline resents the mention of Skye and tells Chloe she will arrange a playdate with Ziggy. Abigail declares she is going to become a vegan, like Bonnie.

Key Happenings

- Wealthy couple, Celeste and Perry White, appear to be happily married and to have it all. However, unbeknownst to anyone else, Perry abuses his wife regularly.

- Madeline Mackenzie is struggling with making her blended family work. She feels that she is losing her fourteen-year-old daughter, Abigail, to her ex-husband, Nathan, and his wife, Bonnie.

Chapters 13-16

Celeste and Perry get in a fight over Perry trying to fix the computer. Perry hits Celeste. Celeste feels she is at fault for asking him to fix the computer. The next day, Celeste tells Perry that she thinks they should try seeing another marriage counselor. He agrees they should go after he gets back from his trip. Perry does not follow through on his promise.

Madeline invites Celeste and her twins to come to the play date with Chloe, Jane, and Ziggy. Madeline remembers how she met Celeste at swimming lessons. Madeline jumped in and pulled Max out from the bottom of the pool when no pool staff was around.

Ziggy and Jane visit Madeline at home. They discuss Jane's move to town. They also discuss Renata's reaction to Amabella's accusation that Ziggy choked her.

Abigail announces that she is spending the night at her father's house. Madeline is angry and upset because Abigail did not consult her first.

Madeline and Ed talk about Jane and Celeste after the play date. Ed says they both seem damaged somehow.

Madeline thinks back to when she was a single mom to Abigail after Nathan left them. She feels hurt and betrayed by Abigail's wish to spend time with Nathan and Bonnie.

Key Happenings

- Celeste and Perry argue after Perry is unable to fix Celeste's computer. Perry hits Celeste, and then promises the next day that he will go with Celeste to see a marriage counselor, but he does not keep his promise.

- Madeline invites Jane and Celeste and their children over for a playdate with her and her daughter Chloe.

- After the playdate. Ed tells Madeline that he thinks both Jane and Celeste seem broken somehow.

Chapters 17-20

Jane's parents go along for Ziggy's first day of school. On the playground before the day starts, Amabella passes out invitations to her birthday party. She gives an invitation to all the children in her class except Ziggy.

Madeline is annoyed about seeing Nathan and Bonnie on the first day of school. When she finds out about the invitations to Amabella's birthday party, she is furious. She tells Renata that Chloe will not be attending the party.

Jane's parents invite Madeline and Ed to join them and Jane at the Blue Blues café. Jane's mother pulls Madeline aside to ask her to help Jane and look out for her. Madeline agrees to do so.

Jane decides she will volunteer to be a parent helper at Ziggy's school. A friend texts Jane that her cousin would like to meet her and asks permission to give him her phone number. Jane agrees. Then she has a panic attack about it and texts her back that she changed her mind. Her friend replies that it is too late.

Key Happenings

- Madeline is upset when she finds out that Amabella and Renata are passing out invitations to Amabella's birthday party to all the children on the playground except Ziggy. She tells Renata that Chloe will not be at the party.

- Jane decides to be a parent helper volunteer at Ziggy's school.

Chapters 21-24

Jane and Celeste decide to start taking walks together while the children are at school.

Madeline's boss at the theater offers her a stack of free front row seat tickets to see *Disney on Ice*. Madeline checks the date and finds out they are for the same day as Amabella's birthday party. She tells her boss she would love to have the tickets.

Perry asks Celeste about Amabella's birthday party. Celeste tells him that Madeline invited her and Ziggy to go to *Disney on Ice* that day instead, and she accepted. She turned down the invitation to Amabella's party. Perry is angry that she did not include him in the *Disney on Ice* trip. He grabs her arm, and then he shoves her. She thinks back about several times in the past when he has abused her.

Eight kindergarten children go to see *Disney on Ice* instead of going to Amabella's birthday party.

After *Disney on Ice,* Jane speaks to her mother on the phone. Her mother, who is curious about Ziggy's paternity, speculates that his father is one of Jane's former boyfriends.

Abigail announces that she would rather live full-time with Nathan and Bonnie than with Madeline and Ed. Madeline is hurt and angry about this decision, but she agrees to it.

Madeline runs into Nathan at athletics day at the school. They speak about Abigail's decision to move in with he and Bonnie. He expresses a concern about money, causing Madeline to become upset over the idea that he might expect her to pay child support to him now.

Key Happenings

- Madeline receives free tickets to *Disney on Ice* from her boss. The show is on the same day as Amabella's party, so Madeline takes Chloe and seven other kindergarteners to the show instead of going to Amabella's party.

- Perry abuses Celeste again when he finds out that she turned down the invitation to Amabella's birthday party without consulting him and excluded him from the *Disney on Ice* trip.

- Abigail decides she would rather live with her father and step-mother than with Madeline and her stepfather.

Chapters 25-28

The kindergarten mothers line up to run in a race on athletics day at the school. Earlier, Abigail told Madeline that she thought Bonnie would win.

Celeste and Renata hold the tape for the runners to cross at the finish line. Celeste is not in the race because she claims she hurt her knee falling down the stairs. She is actually hurt because of a fight between her and Perry the night before. Madeline wins the race just ahead of Bonnie, but Renata claims that Bonnie is the winner. Bonnie and Celeste claim that Madeline is the winner.

Madeline says that Bonnie is the winner and gives her the blue ribbon.

Celeste goes online and spends $25,000 of Perry's money on charities. She is thinking about her relationship with Perry. She rationalizes his behavior by blaming herself for not being grateful enough and for provoking him. Still troubled, she does a search online for information about domestic violence.

Madeline packs Abigail's clothes for her so she can move in with Nathan and Bonnie. Abigail asks to take the four-poster bed that Ed and Madeline gave her for her birthday. Madeline pretends not to care and tells her she can take the bed. Madeline decides to start a book club.

Key Happenings

- Madeline beats Bonnie in a foot race at the school athletics day, but she claims that Bonnie is the winner and gives her the blue ribbon.

- After another fight with Perry, Celeste donates $25,000 of his money to charity. She searches online for information about domestic abuse.

- Madeline acts as if she does not care when she helps Abigail move to Nathan and Bonnie's house, but she feels hurt. To take her mind off of it, Madeline decides to start a book club.

Chapters 29-32

Ziggy needs to do a family tree project for school. Jane gets the due date wrong and realizes her mistake at Ziggy's bedtime the night before the actual due date. Madeline comes to her rescue, bringing her the cardboard they need for the project.

Madeline helps Jane and Ziggy get the family tree project done. Ziggy insists he must write down his father's name in the proper box on the family tree. Jane tells him she does not know his father's name. Madeline tells Ziggy that it is okay for his project to be different from the example the teacher gave them. After Ziggy is in bed and asleep, Jane tells Madeline that Saxon Banks is the name of Ziggy's father.

Jane tells Madeline about the one night stand she had when Ziggy was conceived. Jane was out drinking with her friends. She got drunk and left with an older man named Saxon Banks. They went to his hotel room. As they were about to have sex, he started choking her. She struggled. He took his hands off of her to let her breathe. She told him she did not like that and asked him not to do it again. He ignored her and choked her again. She struggled again. Then he let her breathe, but had sex with her while degrading her for her looks.

Jane had problems with endometriosis when she was younger and did not think she would get pregnant, so she did not take the morning after pill following the one night stand. By the time she realized she was pregnant, it was too late for an abortion.

Madeline is furious thinking about what happened to Jane. Jane accepts responsibility, at least in part for what happened to her. She does not regret having Ziggy. She does wonder if he might have inherited any violent tendencies from his father, but she does not really believe that he has.

Madeline suggests Googling Saxon Banks to see what he is up to now. Jane does not want to and asks Madeline not to do it either. Madeline promises she will not.

Key Happenings

- Madeline comes over to help Jane and Ziggy with a family tree school project due the next day that Jane forgot. Although Jane tells

Ziggy that she does not know his father's name, Jane later tells Madeline that Ziggy's father's name is Saxon Banks.

- Jane tells Madeline how Ziggy was conceived during a one night stand she had with a man named Saxon Banks who attempted to choke her before sex and then verbally abused her during sex. Madeline wants to Google Saxon Banks, but Jane asks her not to do it.

Chapters 33-36

Celeste goes to see a counselor for domestic abuse. She tells the counselor about all that has happened between her and Perry. The counselor tells Celeste that Perry will hit her again and that she needs to develop a plan for when that happens.

Madeline tells Ed Jane's story. He is upset about it, but he says she was silly for letting herself get in that situation. His comment makes Madeline angry because she feels he is blaming Jane for what happened.

Madeline drinks a cup of tea to calm herself down. Then she Googles Saxon Banks even though she promised Jane that she would not. She finds out he is married and has three daughters. She feels bad for searching for the information.

Jane starts taking her laptop to the Blue Blues café during the day to do her work. She has her own accounting business. She makes friends with and is attracted to Tom, the owner, but Madeline tells her that he is gay, so she knows things will go no further between them.

Jane tells Celeste the story of her one-night stand. Jane starts to feel freer, like she is regaining control over her own life, after sharing her secret.

The school principal calls Jane and asks to meet with her. The principal tells Jane that Amabella is being bullied by one of her classmates. Amabella will not tell who is doing it, but Renata believes that Ziggy is responsible. Ziggy claims he did not do it. As the meeting is wrapping up, Jane has an uncomfortable encounter with Renata and her husband, Geof.

Key Happenings

- Celeste sees a domestic abuse counselor who tells her that Perry will hit her again and that she needs to develop a plan for when that happens.

- Madeline goes against her word to Jane and Googles Saxon Banks. She finds out he is married and has three daughters.

- Jane makes friends with Tom, the owner of the Blue Blues cafe. Later she meets with the school principal who tells her that Amabella is being bullied by a classmate, and Renata believes that Ziggy is the one responsible.

Chapters 37-40

Madeline's relationship with Abigail is strained since Abigail moved out to live with her father and stepmother. Madeline finds Abigail looking at the Amnesty International website, reading about child marriage and sex slavery. Madeline thinks Abigail is too young and too sensitive to be thinking about such things. Abigail says she has an idea of how she can do something about it, but she does not tell Madeline what her idea is.

Celeste rents an apartment and furnishes it for herself and her two sons as a way of creating a plan in case she decides to leave Perry. The whole time she is doing it, she is telling herself that she will probably never use it. She is conflicted, thinking about all the good things about her marriage and realizing she will miss those things when she leaves him.

Jane tells Ziggy what the principal told her about Amabella being bullied. She asks Ziggy if it is him. Ziggy tells her that he does not want to talk about it.

Samantha is the first to arrive at Madeline's book club meeting. She tells Madeline that Harper, another kindergarten mother, has started a petition to get Ziggy suspended from school. Chloe tells Madeline that some of the kids are telling Ziggy that they are not allowed to play with him.

Key Happenings

- Celeste secretly rents an apartment where she and her sons can live if she decides to leave Perry.

- When Jane asks Ziggy if he is bullying Amabella, he says he does not want to talk about it.

- At Madeline's book club meeting, the parents talk about how someone has started a petition to get Ziggy suspended from school and how some parents are not allowing their children to play with Ziggy.

Chapters 41-44

Miss Barnes calls Jane just a few minutes before book club is to start and tells her about the petition Harper started against Ziggy.

As Celeste gets ready to go to the book club, her babysitter notices a bruise on her arm. Celeste tells her she got the bruise when she and her tennis partner both went for the same shot.

Ziggy is upset and crying because several children at school have told him that they are not allowed to play with him. He is so upset that Jane decides she cannot go to the book club.

Instead of talking about the book at book club, everyone sits around gossiping and talking about the petition to suspend Ziggy.

Key Happenings

- Kindergarten teacher Miss Barnes calls and tells Jane about the petition that Renata's sidekick, Harper, has started to try and suspend Ziggy from school.

- Ziggy is upset that parents are telling their children not to play with him, so Jane decides to stay home with him instead of going to Madeline's book club.

Chapters 45-48

Madeline and Celeste talk after the book club meeting about Jane's story. Jane told Celeste about the one night stand, but she did not tell her the man's name. Madeline tells her his name, and Celeste recognizes the name as one of Perry's cousin. She decides it is best not to tell Perry about it since they are not sure it is his cousin.

Celeste thinks about Perry's cousin on her way back home. She has always liked Saxon and finds it hard to believe he could have been the one to be so cruel to Jane. Then she realizes that Perry also seems nice to others who do not know his secrets.

Jane takes Ziggy to her parents' house. She tells them about the petition. She considers moving closer to her parents, but realizes she would miss too much about living at Pirriwee Beach.

Madeline checks Abigail's Facebook account. She sees a comment she does not understand from one of Abigail's friends about a project that Abigail is doing. Then she notices that Abigail's reply, telling the friend that the project is top secret, was sent just five minutes earlier. She is upset that Abigail is up late when she is supposed to see her math tutor early the next day. She texts Abigail and tells her to go to bed. Abigail tells her that Nathan canceled the tutor. Madeline is furious that the tutor was canceled without her knowledge and she calls Nathan to express her anger.

Key Happenings

- After the book club meeting, Madeline tells Celeste the name of Jane's one night stand, and Celeste realizes it is the same name as one of her husband's cousins.

- Madeline reads a comment on Abigail's Facebook account about a project that Abigail is doing, but she does not know what it means.

- Madeline is angered when she finds out that Nathan canceled Abigail's math tutor without consulting her first.

Chapters 49-52

Jane stands up to two mothers on the playground who are talking about the petition. She tells them Ziggy has never hurt anyone.

Jane is listening to children read as a parent volunteer. Amabella comes to read to her. Jane asks her if Ziggy is the one who has been hurting her, and Amabella starts to cry. Harper intervenes, claiming that Jane is bullying Amabella just like Ziggy. Jane kicks sand toward Harper and tells her not to talk about Ziggy.

As Madeline and Ed prepare to attend an assembly at the school, Ed learns the editor of the local paper wants him to cover the story of the petition to suspend Ziggy from the school. On the way to the school, they see Celeste and Perry. Jane is not there because she is taking Ziggy to see a psychologist.

Ed and Perry talk about the bullying controversy. Perry asks if he should sign the petition. Celeste tells Perry that if he signs it she will leave him. It is meant as a joke, but it comes out wrong because she sounds serious.

Invitations go out to the parents for the upcoming trivia night. It is to be a costume event with everyone expected to dress up as either Elvis Presley or Audrey Hepburn.

Bonnie sits next to Madeline at the school assembly. Madeline is annoyed as she is reminded once again that Abigail chose to live with Bonnie and Nathan over her and Ed. Bonnie invites them to come to Abigail's fifteenth birthday party, which irritates Madeline even more.

Key Happenings

- Jane, who listens to the children read when she works as a school volunteer, asks Amabella if Ziggy is the one who has been hurting her. The question makes Amabella cry, and Harper claims Jane is a bully just like Ziggy.

- When Perry asks in front of Madeline and Ed if he should sign the petition against Ziggy, Celeste tells him she will leave him if he does. Although she intends it as a joke, it does not go over well because she sounds so serious when she says it.

- Invitations are sent out for the school's trivia night. It is to be a costume event with everyone dressing up as either Elvis Presley or Audrey Hepburn.

Chapters 53-56

The psychologist tells Jane that she does not think Ziggy is a bully or a liar. She tells Jane that he does seem anxious about his father because he thinks his father is someone scary and strange.

When they return home from the school assembly, Perry attacks Celeste. He is outraged because he felt humiliated by her comment saying she would leave him if he signed the petition. He pulls her hair and smashes her head against the wall.

Madeline hears gossip from a friend that Renata's husband, Geoff, is having an affair with their nanny, Juliette. The same friend mentions the charity project Abigail is working on and hints that Madeline should find out more about it.

Perry takes the morning off from work so he can make sure Celeste is all right. Celeste lies in bed and thinks about how he is like Dr. Jekyll and Mr. Hyde. She has thought that once she leaves him, everything will be fine. She now realizes that if she ever leaves him, he will find her and try to kill her.

Key Happenings

- Jane takes Ziggy to see a psychologist. The psychologist does not think Ziggy is a bully or a liar.

- Perry attacks Celeste when they get back home because he feels humiliated by her comment about leaving him. He smashes her head against a wall.

- Celeste is afraid if she tries to leave Perry that he will kill her.

Chapters 57-60

Nathan calls Madeline to tell her that Abigail has built a website to raise funds for Amnesty International. He tells her that Abigail is auctioning off her virginity to raise awareness about child marriage and sex slavery. Abigail is unable to monitor comments. People are leaving lewd comments on the page.

After visiting the psychologist, Jane and Ziggy stop at the Blue Blues café. Harper and her husband come in to the café. Harper's husband comes over to Jane's table and threatens her with a restraining order if she comes near Harper again. Tom makes Harper and her husband leave the café.

Jane asks Ziggy if he knows who has been bullying Amabella. He says he promised Amabella that he would not tell. Jane suggests that he could write the name down instead of telling her, that it would not be breaking his promise to Amabella. Ziggy writes down the name Max, one of Celeste's twins.

Perry gives Celeste a strong painkiller. He has arranged for Madeline to pick up the twins after school so Celeste will not have to do it. As Celeste starts to drift off to sleep, she tries to understand how Perry and his cousin came to be the way they are. She knows Perry was bullied as a child, but Saxon was not, as far as she knows.

Madeline tells Nathan that they need to shut down Abigail's website. Nathan tells her that he cannot shut it down without her login information. They try to guess it, but are unable to figure it out.

Key Happenings

- While living with her father, Abigail creates a website to auction off her virginity in order to support one of Bonnie's favorite charities. Madeline and Nathan try to guess Abigail's login information so they can shut down her website, but they are unable to figure it out.

- When Jane visits the Blue Blues cafe, she is threatened by Harper and her husband. Tom makes Harper and her husband leave the cafe.

- Ziggy informs Jane that the one who has been bullying Amabella is Max, one of Celeste's twins.

Chapters 61-64

Jane takes Ziggy to school after the appointment with the psychologist. She is trying to decide whom she should talk to about Max being the bully. Mrs. Ponder, one of the kindergarten mothers who lives next to the school, speaks to them as they go by her house. She notices Ziggy is scratching his head a lot. She suggests that Ziggy may have lice. Mrs. Ponder checks his head and discovers that he does have lice.

Madeline picks Abigail up from school and tells her she must take her website down. Abigail refuses. They are in the car arguing about it as they get in line at the school to pick up Fred, Chloe, and Celeste's twin boys. Madeline is distracted as they argue, and she runs into the back of Renata's car.

Mrs. Ponder arranges for her daughter, who is a hairdresser, to delouse Ziggy. While they are there, she gives Ziggy and Jane haircuts. She gives Jane a pixie cut that makes her look like Audrey Hepburn.

Madeline drops the twins off at Celeste's house and tells her about Abigail's website.

Key Happenings

- Mrs. Ponder, an older lady who lives next to the school, notices that Ziggy is scratching his head a lot. She checks him for lice and sees that he has them.

- Madeline and Abigail are in the car on the way home from school and are arguing about whether or not Abigail will take her website down. Distracted by the argument, Madeline runs into the back of Renata's car.

- Mrs. Ponder's daughter, a beautician, delouses Ziggy and gives Jane a pixie haircut that makes her look like Audrey Hepburn.

Chapters 65-68

Jane drops Ziggy off at her parents' home so he can spend the day with them. This leaves her free to go to the trivia night later in the evening. On the way home, she stops at Blue Blues café. It is pouring rain, but she decides to go in anyway.

Perry and his sons make breakfast for Celeste the morning of the school trivia night. Perry is scheduled to go to Hawaii for business the next day. Celeste decides she and the boys will move to the apartment while Perry is in Hawaii.

Nathan and Madeline speak with Abigail. They try everything they can think of to get her to take her website down, but she refuses. Ed and Madeline try to figure out a way to get her to take the site down, too. Then Abigail comes and tells them she got an email from a man in South Dakota who says he does not want to bid on her virginity, but he will donate $100,000 if she will take the website down. She tells Ed and Madeline that she has taken the site down.

Jane arrives at Blue Blues café and finds it closed. She is about to leave when Tom comes and lets her in. He closed the café because no one was there because of the rain. Tom lives in the back of the café. He invites her back to his apartment and gets her some dry clothes to wear. During their conversation, Jane finds out that Tom is straight, not gay.

Key Happenings

- Perry is planning a business trip to Hawaii. Celeste decides she and her sons will move out while he is gone.

- While Ed and Madeline are trying to figure out how to get Abigail to take down her website, she comes to tell them that she already took the site down because a man in South Dakota, who does not want to buy her virginity, promised to donate $100,000 if she would take the site down.

- Jane goes to the Blue Blues cafe, but the cafe is closed due to rain when she arrives. Tom invites her in anyway, and while they are talking, Jane finds out that Tom is straight, not gay as she had thought.

Chapters 69-72

While Perry and Celeste are getting ready to go to the trivia night, Josh tells Celeste that Max has stopped hurting Amabella, but now he has pushed Skye down the stairs twice. Celeste is shocked to find out that Max is the bully.

Perry tells Celeste that he received a message for her from her property manager about when the smoke alarms are to be installed. This is his way of telling her that he knows about her secret apartment.

The caterer is delayed on the way to the school trivia night. Everyone is drinking cocktails that are very strong. Someone miscalculated the amount of alcohol when making them so that one drink was as strong as three shots. Parents and teachers are all getting drunk very quickly. Tom, as one of the sponsors of the event, is there. He spends his time talking to Jane. Madeline is excited about seeing them there together.

Celeste and Perry arrive at the trivia night and sit in the car for a few minutes talking before going in. It is raining. Celeste tells Perry that Max is the school bully. She tells him their marriage is over and she will move out with the boys next week while he is gone. Perry is upset and promises he will get help. Celeste has heard it before. She realizes that before she stayed in the relationship because of the kids. Now she realizes she must get out of the relationship because of the kids. Renata comes up to Celeste's car window and interrupts their conversation, asking if they want to share an umbrella.

Bonnie comes up to talk to Madeline at the trivia night. Madeline's inhibitions are gone because of the drinks. She makes several snarky comments to Bonnie regarding Nathan's lack of parenting skills and how Abigail created her website while under their supervision. Bonnie reminds Madeline that it has been fifteen years since Nathan left her and she should think about forgiving him. Right after this Bonnie is bumped from behind by someone and she spills her drink on Madeline. Some who see it think Bonnie threw her drink on Madeline.

Key Happenings

- As Celeste and Perry are getting ready to go to the trivia night, Josh, one of their twins, tells Celeste that his twin Max has bullied both Amabella and Skye, Bonnie and

Nathan's daughter. Perry lets Celeste know that he knows about her secret apartment just before they leave to go to the trivia night.

- Someone accidentally makes the drinks too strong at the trivia night and the parents and teachers are all getting drunk quickly.

- As they arrive at the school, Celeste tells Perry that she and the boys are going to leave him.

Chapters 73-76

Everyone is getting drunker. Miss Barnes comes to check on Jane to see if she is all right. She thinks she may be worrying about the petition. Jane is not even thinking about the petition. All she can think about is the fact that Tom is straight and how attracted she is to him. Celeste comes over to talk to her.

Celeste and Jane go out on the balcony to talk. Celeste apologizes and tells Jane that Max is the bully, not Ziggy. Jane tells her she already knows. Then Nathan and Bonnie join them on the balcony.

Celeste apologizes to them for Max pushing Skye on the stairs. Bonnie tells her they already knew because Skye told them.

Madeline and Renata go out on the balcony, too. Inside things are getting out of control because everyone is getting drunk. Nathan is talking about Abigail's website. Nathan mentions that the donation that caused Abigail to shut down the website came from Perry and Celeste, but Madeline realizes it was from Celeste alone.

Celeste tells Renata that Max is the bully instead of Ziggy. Renata feels terrible and apologizes to Jane.

Ed and Perry join them on the balcony. They bring bar stools with them to sit on. Celeste introduces Perry to Bonnie and Jane. Perry takes off his Elvis wig saying it is itchy. He sits on a bar stool next to the railing. Jane tells Perry that she has met him before, except that he introduced himself then as Saxon Banks.

Perry pretends not to know what she is talking about. Celeste realizes that Perry is Ziggy's father. She throws her drink at him. He angrily slaps her in response. Madeline and Ed rush to protect Celeste. Renata calls the police.

Bonnie seems to change into a different person. She says Perry has hit Celeste before. That is why Max has been hurting little girls. He has watched his father hit his mother. Bonnie is enraged and she pushes Perry. He falls from his bar stool off of the balcony to the ground below.

Key Happenings

- On the balcony at the trivia night, Celeste apologizes to Jane and Bonnie for her son Max's behavior, and Renata apologizes to

Jane for falsely accusing Ziggy of being the bully.

- Jane meets Perry for the first time, and realizes that he is the one she had her one night stand with, but he gave her his cousin's name instead of his own. When Jane confronts him about this, Celeste throws her drink at Perry, and he reacts by slapping her face so hard she is knocked down.

- Enraged, Bonnie pushes Perry off the balcony, and he falls to his death.

Chapters 77-80

Ed tells Renata to call for an ambulance. Renata says that she is, but then she pauses and says that she did not see what happen. Then, one by one, Madeline, Jane, and Celeste say they did not see Perry fall. Bonnie is curled up and crouching on the floor. Nathan is hovering around her. Celeste tells Renata to call an ambulance, and then she begins to scream.

People have begun to fight inside. Two dads crash out onto the balcony and run into Jane and Madeline, knocking them down to the floor.

Madeline, Jane, and several other parents from trivia night are in the hospital the next morning. Ed is visiting Madeline in the hospital. He says he does not think he can cover up for Bonnie. Nathan comes to visit Madeline and tells her Abigail is moving back home to help her out while she is healing. Then Nathan explains to Madeline and Ed that Bonnie's father was violent to Bonnie's mother when Bonnie was a child. Bonnie and her sister saw it all. Bonnie suffers from post-traumatic stress disorder as a result. Madeline reassures Nathan that they will not tell the police what happened.

A policeman takes Jane's statement from her while she is in her hospital bed. She says she did not see what happened to Perry because she was looking inside at the noise and commotion in there. He asks if she is a friend of Perry's. She answers that she met him for the first time that night. The policeman does not believe her.

Bonnie brings a casserole to Celeste and apologizes to her. She tells her she is going to make a statement to the police and tell the truth. She says the others do not need to lie for her and cover up the truth. It was an accident.

Key Happenings

- Bonnie, whose father was abusive to her mother when she was a child, snapped when she realized Perry abuses Celeste and that Max has learned this abuse from watching him. This is why she pushed Perry off the balcony.

- After Perry's death, everyone pretends they do not know what happened. However, Bonnie decides to confess so the others will not have to lie for her.

- Madeline, Jane, and some of the other parents end up in the hospital because of the brawling that went on at the trivia night.

Chapters 81-84

Celeste texts Madeline and tells her that Bonnie is going to confess. Madeline calls Ed to give him the message.

Renata writes a letter to Ziggy to apologize. She and Amabella are moving to London. She invites him to Amabella's going away party.

Jane allows Ziggy to go with her to Perry's funeral. Even though he does not know it at the time, he is attending his father's funeral. She wants to be able to tell him the whole story when he is older. A video at the funeral portrays Perry as a loving father, husband, and family man. Jane tries to think of Perry that way and tries to forget the other side of him that she has seen.

Jane and Tom take a walk on the beach together. They share a lunch and then he kisses her.

A journalist talks to everyone she can about what happened at the school trivia night and about the events leading up to it. She is writing a book. The pieces of the puzzle fit together as seen from various viewpoints.

Celeste continues her counseling to try to sort out her feelings. Part of her still loves and misses Perry. Part of her is furious with him for cheating on her, for the way he abused her, and for what he did to Jane. She sells her house and moves with her sons to the apartment she rented. She goes back to work. Trust funds have been set up for her sons, and she also sets one up for Ziggy since he is Perry's son, too.

Bonnie is sentenced to community service instead of jail time.

Celeste gives a speech to health professionals about domestic abuse. She begins her speech by saying that it can happen to anyone.

Key Happenings

- Jane and Ziggy attend Perry's funeral service, because Jane feels it is appropriate for Ziggy to attend his father's funeral even though she will not reveal his identity to him until he is older. Later, Jane and Tom take a walk on the beach and share a lunch and a kiss.

- Bonnie confesses to the police what she has done and is sentenced to community service.

- Celeste sells the house she shared with Perry and moves with her boys to the apartment she had rented. She goes back to work, continues counseling, and helps others by giving speeches about domestic violence.

A Reader's Perspective

Big Little Lies by Liane Moriarty is a clever murder mystery that keeps the reader guessing until the end, not only about who the murderer is, but also about who the victim is. Moriarty weaves together the lives and friendships of three very different mothers whose children are all in the same kindergarten class. With the combination of memorable characters, suspense, and humor, Moriarty skillfully pulls her readers along through the story, making them eager to know what is going to happen next.

The story is told through multiple voices and viewpoints. Throughout the novel are short comments from various people who live on the Pirriwee Peninsula where the story takes place. These comments provide clues to the mystery and add details to the story that the reader would otherwise not know. It is not until close to the end of the story that the reader realizes these comments are snippets of interviews given to a journalist who is writing a story about the murder.

Moriarty handles the themes of motherhood, marriage, family, infidelity, and domestic abuse with compassion, wit, and a dramatic flair. The characters are quirky, but genuine, as they struggle with the secrets and lies in their lives.

Jane is a single mother trying to do her best to provide for her son while at the same time healing from her troubled past. When her son, who was born as a result of a one-night stand with a stranger, is accused of being the school bully, she wonders if he has inherited a violent nature from his father.

Madeline tries to be there for everyone in a balancing act between standing up for her friends and taking care of her blended family. She wants to be a good wife and mother, but she must get over feeling hurt and jealous when her teenage daughter chooses to live with her ex-husband and his new, younger wife instead of with Madeline and her current husband.

Celeste's life seems perfect to her friends and the people in the community. She is beautiful, wealthy and has an attentive husband and twin sons. Those who see her assume she is happily married. They do not know that the secret she keeps hidden is one of domestic violence.

Although, for the most part, the characters ring true and the plot seems believable, one subplot is somewhat difficult to believe. Madeline's teenage daughter decides she wants to draw awareness to child marriage and sexual slavery as well as find a way to contribute to Amnesty International. To do this, she decides to auction off her virginity on the internet. She then plans to donate the money that is raised to Amnesty International. It seems highly unlikely, in the current-day, digital world where teens have grown up knowing about and using computers since they were toddlers, that a bright, fourteen-year-old girl would come up with this idea and not consider what the consequences of such an action would be. If the reader can suspend disbelief about this subplot, the rest of the story is easy to imagine. Readers will recognize themselves, their neighbors, their family, and their friends in the mostly well-intentioned but imperfect and struggling characters in *Big Little Lies*.

Moriarty manages to pull everything together and tie in all the loose ends in the rollicking conclusion at the school's fundraiser. No one would have guessed that a murder could occur at the unlikely occasion of a costume party trivia night where parents and teachers dress as Elvis Presley and Audrey Hepburn while nearly everyone present is drunk. However, Moriarty makes it work to the delight and amusement of the reader.

~~~~~~~~ END OF SUMMARY~~~~~~~~

Thank you for purchasing this summary. We hope you enjoyed it. If so,

please leave a review. We are interested in talking to you to learn how we can improve! Please email instaread.summaries@gmail.com with "Survey" in the subject field to take a quick survey. We will send you a $5 gift card from the store of your choice upon completion of the survey! -:)

Made in the USA
San Bernardino, CA
31 January 2015